ISBN 0-7683-2103-4

Written by Flavia and Lisa Weedn
Illustrated by Flavia Weedn
© Weedn Family Trust
www.flavia.com
All rights reserved

Published in 1999 by Cedco Publishing Company
100 Pelican Way, San Rafael, California 94901
For a free catalog of other Cedco® products, please write
to the address above, or visit our website: www.cedco.com

Library of Congress Cataloging-in-Publication Data

Weedn. Flavia.
    Flavia and the Christmas legacy / written by Flavia & Lisa Weedn;
illustrated by Flavia Weedn.
        p. cm.
    Summary: A gentle Christmas story reminds us that love is the greatest
gift of all and that it is the very legacy we give our children, so they will
have it to give to their own.
    ISBN 0-7683-2103-4
    [1. Christmas--Fiction. 2. Family life--Fiction.] I. Weedn, Lisa, 1959-
II. Title.
PZ7.W4145Fl 1999
[E]----dc21
                                      99-10324
                                      CIP

Printed in Hong Kong

1 3 5 7 9 10 8 6 4 2

The artwork for each picture is digitally mastered using acrylic on canvas.

*With love and gratitude to those talented souls who made this book a reality—
Rick Weedn, Lisa Mansfield, Diana Musacchio, Jane Durand, Tyler Tomblin,
Heather Day, Solveig Chandler, Hui-Ying Ting-Bornfreund, Annette Berlin.*

Flavia and the CHRISTMAS LEGACY

A S T O R Y

WRITTEN BY FLAVIA AND LISA WEEDN
ILLUSTRATED BY FLAVIA WEEDN

Cedco Publishing • San Rafael, California

Some called her Mama,
some called her Gramma Syl,
but she was an angel, and her magic
touched the earth for awhile.

It is with love that we dedicate
this book to her.

SYLVIA MAE MONEY

1906-1979

And to Willie and Judy,
who share the memories.

It was the day before Christmas Eve, and cold, as Flavia and her younger brother, Willie, walked down the street looking into store windows. It was a magical time of year because the sights and sounds of Christmas were everywhere. Flavia even thought she could taste Christmas in the air.

The family had drawn names for Christmas last Thanksgiving when they were all together, and now Flavia and Willie were trying to find just the right gifts for the names they had chosen.

Flavia knew it wouldn't be easy this year because there was very little money to spend, and since she had drawn Willie's name she was trying very hard to keep him from knowing.

She knew this was all part of the excitement and magic that had always happened this time of year for as long as she could remember. The magic was because of Mama. Everyone knew it was Mama's most favorite time, and since Flavia and Willie believed Mama to be an angel, Christmas, no matter what, had always been very important and very wonderful at their house.

Flavia looked up at the calendar on the kitchen door, where she and Willie had been marking the days, and saw that now there were only two days left. She felt a tingling inside when she thought of Christmas . . . and quietly wished that everyone in the world could share this wonderful feeling.

It was almost dark now, and she looked at everything around her. Mammo, her grandmother, was cutting out gingerbread cookies, while Daddy tried to untangle the Christmas lights.

The room was still cold from when Daddy had opened the door and brought in the Christmas tree. Flavia saw how small the tree was this year and knew it would have to be put on the table instead of the floor. She wondered if Willie noticed.

Mama was baking bread dough stars for the tree and trying to make a cloth doll at the same time. Flavia's young uncle, Jack, had just hung the sleigh bells outside on the front door, and returned to the back room of the house where he would often go to write.

Jack was very special to her, and when she knew he was writing, she never bothered him, for she knew that words don't come easy sometimes.

Jack wrote poems and stories about how he felt inside . . . and how being alive was magic. He was very wise and a lot like a big brother to her. Jack knew about dreams and not giving up and about believing. He knew about all the wonderful things. He was a Dream Maker.

*F*lavia looked across the room at the someone new this Christmas . . . for now there was a little baby sister, Judy. While Judy was sleeping, Flavia put a tiny doll inside the bassinet and wondered what Judy would think when she woke up and saw it, and whether or not she would ever love dolls the way Flavia did.

Willie brought the Christmas Picture Book down from the shelf, and he and Flavia lay on the floor and slowly began to look at the pages. They loved looking at photographs of other Christmases, and as they turned the pages they talked softly about how it was just like turning pages in time. Willie asked, "Why aren't there any pictures of Santa Claus in this whole book? If there aren't any pictures of him, how do we know what he really looks like?"

Mama smiled and said, "Close your eyes, Willie, and you can *picture* him. Use the magic in your mind . . . your imagination . . . and you can see him. Just *picture* how you think Santa Claus should look, and what he really is to you. He may look different to each of us, but if you try real hard and believe you can do it, you will see him, I promise. Begin by remembering that he is someone very special because he gives to others."

    The room was quiet for a few minutes, then Daddy began
to tell Flavia and Willie where he had been when he wasn't in
some of the pictures in the book, and about what he had
learned on the Christmases he'd been away.

    He told them how, in some other countries, people
celebrated different holidays and that not everyone, even in
this country, celebrated Christmas. "There are religions in this
country and in others where people believe differently and
celebrate with different kinds of food and songs and stories,"
he said, "and their traditions mean as much to them as
Christmas does to us."

    Daddy had been gone a lot, and had lived and worked all
over the world. He knew all about holidays and customs and
things far away, and had a special way of talking about the
places he'd been. When he described them, it always made
Flavia think she was really there.

    She knew that meant she was using her imagination, and
she loved it when she could imagine being in some of the
places he talked about. He said it was just like going on a
magic carpet ride. And to her it was, for that is how Flavia
saw the world.

As Flavia looked at the photographs again, she saw how even some of their own Christmases had been different from the rest. It was all there in the book. Some Christmases had tall trees and lots of wrapped presents, and some had little trees and few presents. Sometimes Mama made stars for a manzanita branch, put the branch in a clay pot, and that had been their tree.

There were pictures of Christmases when Flavia and Willie had been babies, and some even before they had been born. Seeing these gave her a funny feeling . . . because Flavia could never imagine this world without her in it.

But the Christmas she remembered most was not one pictured in the book. It was the Christmas when Mama had made Flavia a coat from Mama's own coat. There was no money to spend that Christmas and so it was Flavia's only present under the tree. Flavia knew now that the number of presents wasn't important . . . and that the real gift was knowing that Mama loved her that much.

Whenever she thought of times like this, tears came to her eyes and a feeling came over her as though the love she felt inside would overflow . . . and she knew she would always have these times to remember, just like those photographs in the book.

She was thinking how much she cared about all the people around her, and how she wished she could stop time and hold it in her hands so that she could keep things just the way they were at that very moment . . . forever.

It was a feeling she had felt often since Jack told her that what she was feeling was a gift and that it would be a part of her for as long as she lived.

Every time she felt this way, Flavia wanted to be near Mama.

Mama was still sewing the doll, so Flavia sat closely down beside her. She often would sit next to Mama while she sewed, and they would talk about things.

Mama knew all about dolls and imaginations, for she was a dollmaker. She made them out of cloth scraps and buttons and yarns and ribbons and lace and threads. But somehow they all looked like people when she was finished. *Real people.*

Sometimes Flavia would talk to them, dance with them and pretend they were real. Mama made all kinds of dolls, and every year she made angel dolls . . . but the angel doll Mama was making now was the most beautiful Flavia had ever seen.

In her long angel hair there was a wreath woven of shiny gold ribbons, and her dress was white and filmy and full. Mama had sewn a tiny satin ribbon on the dress and little gold stars on the hem.

Flavia looked at the angel doll lovingly for a long time before she asked, "Who is it for, Mama? Is it a present?"

"Who it's for is a secret," Mama said, "but it is for someone who will understand what Christmas really means. It is a special doll, a Christmas Angel Doll . . . and it is filled with love."

While Mama spoke, Flavia saw her glance over at the bassinet and look at little Judy. Then Flavia heard her own thoughts inside, as though they had a voice, and the voice inside was telling her that Mama was making the doll for Judy.

When Flavia looked at the sleeping baby and saw how little she was and how she looked like a baby angel, Flavia understood why Mama would surely give it to her.

And then Flavia heard her thoughts tell her something else . . . she would have to remember that from now on Mama would love Judy just as much as she loved Willie and her. With that thought, Flavia quickly turned her head so that Mama could not see the tears that filled her eyes.

That night before she fell asleep, Flavia remembered how the Christmas tree was little again and how Christmas would be even more different this year because there was a baby sister.

Flavia also wondered if there would be any special gifts for her or Willie, now that they had to share with someone new. There had always been one special gift under the tree for each of them, and they were always a little different than the rest.

These were the gifts that were set aside to be opened later on Christmas night, after all the rest of the family had gone home.

Then Flavia remembered Willie's questions about Santa Claus, so she closed her eyes and tried to *picture* him. No matter how many times she began to imagine him, the pictures in her mind always turned Santa Claus into someone who looked a lot like The Hanky Man . . . that special man who gathered up broken toys and things, repaired them, and gave them to children.

Except for the red jacket and the long white beard that Santa was supposed to have, they looked just the same. There was something else Flavia thought of. How did The Hanky Man always seem to know which toys each child wished for? Maybe he really was Santa Claus. Maybe, when he wasn't in the North Pole, he drove this old red truck down the alley of their street every Tuesday collecting broken toys to fix.

Maybe underneath his red coat, Santa wore an old shirt and red suspenders. And maybe he played a harmonica and sang gypsy songs so full of joy and wonder that it made Willie and her eager for Tuesdays to come. She was still thinking about all the maybes when she fell asleep.

*I*t was after breakfast on Christmas Eve morning, and Mama and Mammo sat at the kitchen table working. Mama was decorating her bread dough stars for the tree, and Mammo was putting icing on the Christmas cookies.

Flavia and Willie listened while Mama told them about when she was a little girl and what her own Papa had taught her. He had told her that *giving* was a gift itself . . . and once you understood it, you never forgot what it meant. And that love was the very best gift of all.

Flavia watched Mama's face as she spoke and her hands as they worked. She thought about how lucky she was to have her. Mama knew more than just about dolls and imaginations. She knew about *giving* and about love, just like her Papa before her, and Flavia knew that that made Mama strong. Flavia hurried to tell Willie what she was sure of now . . . both Mama and her Papa before her were angels.

While Flavia and Willie were hanging their stockings alongside Judy's, Willie said, "Flavia, I've been thinking about what Mama said, and how to *picture* Santa Claus, and I keep *picturing* him to be just like The Hanky Man. So, I've been wondering, could Santa drive a red truck all year long, and a sleigh with reindeer only at Christmastime? Could his truck become the sleigh, the way Cinderella's pumpkin became a coach?" Willie's eyes widened at the thought of all that wonder.

Flavia didn't tell Willie how her thoughts had been much the same as his the night before. It was Tuesday, and they both knew The Hanky Man would come by today to gather more things to fix and then give away. But Flavia knew they couldn't ask him about all they had been thinking. This was something she would have to talk to Jack about, because she was sure that all Dream Makers knew about things this wonderful.

But, for now, the questions would go unanswered, so she busied herself again with the mistletoe and tying it with a ribbon, while Willie put the star on top of the tree, then quietly took a handful of Christmas candy from the tall glass jar on the table.

Suddenly Flavia thought of something, and reached to peek inside the box that had been filled and was waiting for The Hanky Man. She wondered if just maybe Mama could be giving the Christmas Angel Doll to The Hanky Man so that he could give it to "someone who understood what Christmas really meant!"

Although it wasn't in the box, Flavia kept wondering and thinking about the doll. She quietly wished she had asked Mama, even before the Christmas Angel Doll was finished, if she could have held it just once.

That night, after Jack had finished his writing, he waited with Flavia and Willie on the street corner until the church's big truck picked them up. Willie was very excited as Jack helped him climb into the back of the open truck.

It would be Willie's first time caroling, and it made him feel very tall. Jack told them both to watch the people's faces as they sang to them.

Willie thought Jack meant they would be surprised, but Flavia remembered something Jack had said to her. "You can see a lot when you look into people's faces. Their feelings and their lives are written there."

With this on her mind, Flavia began to see something different this year. As they sang Christmas songs, she saw a kind of glow come over the people's faces and she realized that by singing for them they were giving them something magic. This *giving* made her feel good inside, just like Mama had said.

Later that night, she looked out the window and talked to
the moon about all that had happened this day. For a long time
now, the moon had been a kind of special friend to her, and
before she would go to sleep at night, she'd often think out loud
and tell the moon things she secretly thought and dreamed
of . . . and about all the wonder she thought was in the world.

The moon and Jack had always listened, no matter what,
and now she was unafraid to tell or ask them anything.
Sometimes she wondered if Willie also talked to the moon at
night. She knew sometimes he talked to one of the cloth rabbits
Mama had made. She had heard him.

Christmas, it was here!

Flavia could not remember when they had not had a *crumble-up* breakfast on Christmas morning, and this year she was glad it was the same. *Crumble-up* meant the crumbling of bacon over biscuits and milk gravy.

There were also scrambled eggs and *chow-chow*, the sauce Daddy made with tomatoes and onions and chili peppers.

Flavia didn't like the *chow-chow* much. Her favorite was Mama's biscuits spread with the apricot jam Mammo made.

The opening of gifts came after breakfast, and then in the early afternoon the aunts and uncles and cousins came over, along with some of their neighbors, like Mrs. Spurgeon, who otherwise would have been alone on Christmas.

They all spent the day talking and laughing and taking pictures and singing and telling stories and just being together.

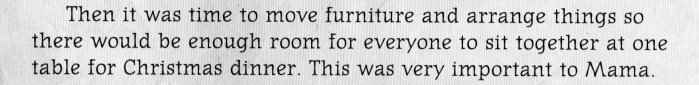

Then it was time to move furniture and arrange things so there would be enough room for everyone to sit together at one table for Christmas dinner. This was very important to Mama.

Flavia and Willie helped Jack, as he shoved three different tables together and covered them with tablecloths so that it would look like one long table.

Flavia wished the chairs were all alike, the way they always were in the pictures in magazines, but those thoughts quickly left her mind when she saw how wonderful Mama had made the table look.

Mama had covered oranges with cloves, wrapped them all in ribbons, and put one at every plate. It made the whole room smell even more like Christmas.

The dinner of turkey, cornbread dressing, yams, a salad made of apples and walnuts, and everything else Flavia looked forward to each year was on that table.

After the pumpkin pie and Christmas cookies, the day turned into night and the rest of the family and the neighbors began to leave.

Flavia wondered why it always took Christmas such a long time to get here, and then it was over so soon.

But inside she knew it wasn't really over, not yet. In fact, the time she most waited for was now, when everyone else had gone home and it was just them . . . the time for Flavia and Willie's special gifts to be opened, the ones that had been set aside for Christmas night.

And this year one more gift had been added, the one for baby Judy.

Willie opened his present first. It was a snow globe with angels and stars, all sparkly and filled with wonder. After Willie turned it upside down and shook it, the snow began to fall over the angels' wings and shine like magic.

When Flavia looked at it, she imagined she was one of those angels and was dancing on a cloud up by the moon, and that the stars were dancing around her like snowflakes. It was a wonderful feeling.

Then Flavia made her quiet wish and began to open her gift. And there it was, wrapped in tissue, the present she had secretly dreamed and hoped for . . . the Christmas Angel Doll Mama had made.

She was the one Mama had been thinking of, the "someone who would understand what Christmas really means."

She held it close to her heart, looked up at Mama's beautiful face, and felt so full of love she could not speak.

The last gift was for baby Judy. Hers was small, wrapped in an envelope tied with a golden ribbon.

Jack reached for it under the tree, untied the ribbon and slipped the page out of the envelope.

It was the poem he had been writing on Christmas Eve. He had titled it "The Christmas Legacy," and he began to read . . .

THE
CHRISTMAS LEGACY

The lights are dim

but atop the tree

a star is shining bright.

For in spite of

closing darkness

it's Christmas Eve tonight.

And small hands clasp

at a doll's soft curl

and small eyes open wide.

And a small heart

thrills with happiness

at the presents

side by side.

But dear little one,

the things you have

are more than

those you see.

The real gifts

at this Christmastime

are not placed on

the tree.

A family close

in love and joy,

the care that they

can give,

the promise

you shall always have,

this country in which

to live.

Each may have

his presents,

but yours are more

precious, dear . . .

for you give love

and hope anew,

and you give it

by just being here.

When Jack finished reading, his poem had so described the feelings of all the people in the room that tears came to every face.

Then there was a long silence, while the lights on the tree made Mama's bread dough stars suddenly twinkle.

More magic, Flavia thought.

As she put her head to her pillow that night, Flavia could hear Mama rocking Judy to sleep.

But Mama was singing something new tonight, for she had given a tune to the poem Jack had written and was singing it like a song.

Flavia knew what Mama had meant now . . . that *giving* was the real spirit of Christmas.

She also knew that the Christmas Angel Doll, which she held onto so tightly now, she would one day give to her own daughter.

And she understood that *giving*, like love, is a gift . . . and the only way to keep love forever is to give it away.

Flavia gave a long last look up into the night and saw the Christmas sky and the magic of the moon and stars above her. She heard the faint sound of sleigh bells and began to wonder whether it was coming from the front door or from somewhere in the night sky.

She then smiled and realized it really didn't matter from where the sound was coming, it only mattered that she had heard it.

As she closed her eyes, she thought of all the love and wonder that had been given that Christmas and she hoped she would never forget this night.

Flavia didn't know that by this time, having finished rocking the baby, Mama was now standing at the half-open door and heard her as she said her prayers.

And she didn't see Mama smile or the tear of love that rolled down her cheek when she heard Flavia softly whisper, just before she fell asleep . . .

Epilogue

Flavia would always remember that very special Christmas . . . and years later she and Willie and Judy would each sing the song Mama had sung, the one from Jack's poem. They would sing it to their own children while rocking them to sleep.

Flavia would still make bread dough stars for the manzanita branch and would give an angel doll to her daughter every Christmas. And sometimes, Flavia would still talk to the moon.

On that Christmas night so long ago, Flavia could not have known that her life would become a gift woven of hopes and dreams, and that it would always be filled with love and surprises.

But most of all, she could not have known then what she knows now . . . that love is more than a gift, it is a most precious legacy. A legacy we give our children, so that they will have it to give to their children.

Love does indeed live forever, for it is a part of the wonder and the magic that is spilled upon this earth.

Merry Christmas, dear world.

Bread Dough Stars

4 Cups Flour
1 Cup Salt
1 Cup Water

Preheat oven to 350 degrees.

Mix ingredients together with your hands. If mixture is too dry or stiff, slowly add a little more water.

After thoroughly mixing, knead dough for 4 to 5 minutes.

Using a rolling pin, roll the dough out like pie crust.

Use star-shaped cookie cutters to form stars in dough. For more magically shaped stars, use an ordinary table knife and draw stars into the dough.

Near the top of each star, use a pencil to make a hole large enough so that gold cord, ribbon, or fishing line can be strung through to make a hanger.

Bake for approximately one hour. Make sure to check for doneness with toothpick. You'll know the stars are ready when the dough is no longer soft.

After stars have cooled on wax paper, apply glue that dries clear and sprinkle with glitter.

Tie ribbon, gold cord or fishing line though the hole in each star and hang on tree.

Note: Bread dough stars are for decorative purposes only and are not meant to be eaten.